Arrowhead

Sheila Crust

Contents

Prologue 1

Chapter 1 7

Chapter 2 11

Chapter 3 16

Chapter 4 20

Chapter 5 24

Chapter 6 28

Chapter 7 33

Chapter 8 41

Chapter 9 45

Chapter 10 51

Chapter 11 58

Chapter 12 66

Prologue

Mom had finally done it eight months ago. She finally left her abusive husband behind and had left with me to start a new life halfway across the country. It took her finding out she was pregnant with my baby brother to get her to leave, but she still finally did it. I couldn't wait to have a sibling despite our 22 year age gap.

Here we were all these months later and my mom had gone into labor. When we arrived at the hospital, they had a wheelchair waiting for us at the ER because I thankfully remembered to call ahead. Mom was all I had in the world since my dad died when I was six months old. I don't think she ever got over his death and that led her to make some bad decisions, but she was still my mom and she always loved me unconditionally.

Mom's screams of pain really worried me. I was terrified I would lose her, my brother, or both of them. But Mom needed me to be strong for her right now, so I was. I allowed her to crush my hand through painful contractions and I tried to help her regulate her breathing. I wiped sweat from her forehead with a cool washcloth. I encouraged her as much as I could and told her that she could do anything. She looked at me with love-filled eyes and I knew it was her way of thanking me right now.

"Mrs. Kingsley, we need you to push one last time. One very hard final push!" Her doctor ordered. Mom gritted her teeth, clamped down on my hand, took a deep breath, and screamed as she strained to push as hard as she could. We were rewarded with tiny little cries as my brother made his grand appearance.

The doctor looked at me and asked if I wanted to cut his umbilical cord. With absolutely no hesitations, I grabbed the metal scissors from her glove-covered hands and cut it with tears streaming down my face. I finally had a lifelong best friend. I got a good glimpse of his face before they took him over to the scale and sink. He was the most beautiful thing I have ever seen.

After I handed back the scissors, I looked at my mom again to tell her how beautiful he was. I had barely gotten the words out of my mouth when I noticed something was horribly wrong. Mom was too pale and she looked like she was barely breathing and that's when I heard her heart monitor flatline.

My heart skipped a beat, my breath got stuck in my throat, and my blood ran cold. I tried telling myself this wasn't happening, but the yelling from the nurses and doctors brought me back to my harsh new reality.

"Sir, you need to get out of the room now!" I was frozen in place. "Now! Go look after your brother while we work on your mother. We need space to work and he needs skin-to-skin contact! GO!" I was torn; I didn't want to leave my mother to die alone if she wasn't going to make it nor did I want my brother to spend his first moments out of the womb alone with strangers.

In the end, I was shoved out of the room and yanked to where ever my baby brother was. I was numb and in shock until I saw his little face. The nurse had me take my shirt off and sit down in a recliner. Five minutes later, he was placed on my chest in nothing but a diaper with a little blanket around him and a tiny hat on his head. I held him close, kissed the top of his head, and allowed my tears to fall. Would my mom even get to hold my brother once? Was it too late? What went wrong?

Screams filled the air as much as smoke did as everyone was running out of the pack house. Thank the Moon Goddess for our heightened senses! That was the only thing saving all my pack members from engulfing in flames. I was waiting by the door to make sure all members had evacuated the premises before I moved towards them. Once the last warrior cradling a little girl to his chest ran towards her parents, I knew we all made it out alive. My pack and I watched our pack house burn to the ground. We couldn't stop it if we tried as it was a magical fire that would only stop once the house was fully in ashes.

I was angry as hell. Not only had I lost my childhood home filled with my parents' belongings, my pack had also been threatened in the worst of ways. I had to force my wolf, River, down because he was raging to take control.

"Not now, River. I'll let you out for a run later, but our pack needs me right now," I told him through our mind-link. He scowled at me before blocking me from his mind.

Using my Alpha voice, I boomed out, "Burrow Hills Pack, we have been a victim of arson. While I don't know who was behind this cowardly attack yet, I vow to you all that I WILL find the dirty bastards who did this. I will find them and I will kill them all with no mercy."

My Beta and best friend, Atlas, came up beside me and assured everyone he was as serious as I was. We wouldn't stop looking for whomever did this and we would wage war until they surrendered or were all killed. I looked at him with a confident expression on my face as I nodded along to his words. He was a damn good Beta, but he was an even better friend.

"Alpha Rafferty, where are we going to stay now?" One of my pack members asked almost hesitantly.

"No worries, Shannon. I had Beta Atlas mind-link the Alpha and Beta of the Godric's Hollow Pack while the fire was burning. We are allowed to stay there for a few days until I can think of something more permanent." I gave her a small smile.

My pack looked exhausted. The children were silently crying and everyone had black ash on our clothes. It was a horrid sight to see

and it fueled my anger. Fires were devastating in so many ways and I
was determined to make whomever did this pay.

"Let's all make our way to Godric's Hollow now. They'll be expecting
us and we all need to sleep. We've had a hard day, but we all survived
because that s what we do. We survive and fight back. Don't be
afraid to let your emotions out, either. We ALL lost our house and
some belongings that can never be replaced, but we WILL come back
stronger than ever when we rebuild." I said my last words for the time
being.

I just wanted to get to Godric's Hollow and get everyone situated, so
I could let River out. He unblocked me and had been angry pacing
in my mind ever since. I knew why he was so angry because I felt the
same way, too. We're the Alpha of our pack and we failed to protect
ourselves against this attack. We couldn't save our home. We failed
today, but I vowed to redeem ourselves and I NEVER break a vow.
Ever. Neither does River.

Chapter 1

It's been six weeks since my life forever changed. I went from being a soon-to-be big brother to being a single father in the blink of an eye. The doctors said the placenta detached itself from my mom's womb and she bled to death in minutes. There wasn't anything they could do. I don't know what kills me more; the fact that I didn't get to say goodbye or that she never got to hold her new baby boy.

Mom and I had been living in a shelter throughout her pregnancy to try and save money to rent a small apartment by the time the baby was born. Unfortunately, Mom had a high risk pregnancy and was eventually put on bed rest, so she couldn't work. I got a job as a night auditor at a nice hotel called the Arrowhead Inn when she was five months pregnant. Between Mom's doctor appointments, buying food. and trying to get everything needed for the baby, it was hard to save and I still barely had anything to show for it.

When the owner of the Arrowhead Inn learned that my mother had died during childbirth, he had made a deal with me. I was allowed to move into the worker's suite connected to the front desk with my baby brother as long as I was okay with earning one paycheck a month. The other paycheck I'd normally get counted as my rent money. With nowhere else to go, I jumped at the offer and agreed to move in when I started to back to work.

I had gotten Mom cremated because it was the cheapest option and I also wanted her with us always. Besides, we didn't know anyone here in Kansas City, so she didn't need a funeral. After my mom died, the hospital's social worker called me into a meeting. She asked about what I wanted to do with my brother. I looked at her incredulously and said, "he's staying with me. I'll take care of him." I explained the situation involving his biological father and she agreed that he didn't need to know a thing. Since Mom had died, his birth certificate noted that his mother was deceased and his father was me, Kenzo James Carson. I named him Kenji Michael Carson and we stopped being brothers that day. He became my son and I became his dad. I promised to love, support, and protect him for the rest of our lives and I was determined to do anything to make him happy.

I was graciously granted six weeks of unpaid paternity and bereavement leave after Kenji was born that ended today. Tonight was my last night off for who knows how long. I couldn't believe that time was already up, but I was also glad it was. I needed to start making money fast because diapers, wipes, and formula were NOT cheap and the cash I had saved was dwindling. I just hoped that I could get Kenji on a good schedule, so I could get all my work done within the hours of my shift. The last thing we needed was for me to lose my job and get us kicked out of our suite, but I wouldn't ever let that happen, not when my newborn son was counting on me.

The best part of living and working here at the Arrowhead Inn was that I never had to leave my baby boy with a babysitter. I was able to find a nice baby monitor set and a baby carrier at a thrift store for great prices. I also was given a matching stroller and car seat set and a playpen from the hospital Kenji was born at. As much as I hate people's pity, there was nothing I'd ever turn down for Kenji. My pride and ego would never get in the way of providing for him.

I really wanted to start saving up money, but with only getting one paycheck a month, I knew that'd be hard, so I planned on talking to my boss tomorrow to see if I could also become the maintenance man around here. I had heard our old one quit, so I immediately decided I'd ask if I could do it since my other job was during the night. It wouldn't be a whole lot more than I'm making now, but I needed every single penny I could get my hands on.

Chapter 2

It has been six weeks since the fire that burnt our pack house to the ground. We stayed with the Godric's Hollow Pack for a week before I came up with a game plan.

I had organized a meeting between my Beta, Delta, Head Warrior, Head Tracker, Head Omega, and all their respective mates. That's right; all of them had found their mates and here I was alone. I felt the void in my heart grow deeper. "I want my mate," growled River through our mind-link. Duh, so did I, but there are other things to worry about right now. My wolf must've heard my thoughts because he mentally flipped me off and blocked me. I sighed deeply and rubbed my temples. It was times like these that I yearned for my mate the most. For someone to help me carry the weight of the pack on their shoulders.

"Rafa, are you okay? Do you want to push this meeting back a bit?"
The Head Omega, Beatrice, asked while giving my hand a squeeze.
Leave it to my Omega to check in on me first, but then again, she's
known me all my life, so she's like a second mother to me. I smiled a
small, genuine smile for the first time in weeks and squeezed her hand
back. Goddess, they had such pure hearts. Some packs treated their
Omegas like scum, but not this pack. In this pack, anyone could be
who they wanted; an Omega could be a Warrior and a Warrior could
cook dinner every night if one so desired.

"I'm fine, Bea. Thank you for asking. Now, if I could all, please, have
your attention!" I said, not even bothering to use my Alpha voice.
I don't need to when it's just us. Years of friendship and trust have
solidified and cemented enough that formality doesn't always need
to be present in our private meetings.

When everyone fell silent and looked at me, I began to unfold my
plans. "What do you all think about completely booking and renting
all the rooms at the Arrowhead Inn for an undetermined length of
time while we build a new pack house? We have plenty of money
in our pack savings, not to mention the insurance money that will

nearly triple our money altogether, so that won't be an issue." I looked around expectantly.

Beta Atlas cocked his head to the side in thought before saying, "Rafa, I think that's a great idea! The Arrowhead Inn isn't very far from our land, which means it's not far from the schools the children in our pack attend." I thanked him for his contribution.

"I third this motion. Being close to our land and home will be good for everyone. If we settle too far, even temporarily, many will get homesick." Beatrice's mate, Elaine, added. To be honest, I didn't even think of that, but she's right. She was so damn right. This was exactly why I had Head Omegas. They were naturally calming and healing, so they always offered a perspective or idea as to how keep the pack from getting too distraught.

"I think staying at the Arrowhead Inn is a smart plan because we'll be able to keep an eye on our land in case of future attacks and we'll be able to train every day still." My Head Warrior, Samuel, added. Now, that I had thought of when I chose the Inn, but I love it when my team already knows part of the reason why I chose something.

"Plus, us Trackers will be able to work on catching scents and leads, so we can find the sons of bitches who did this to us," Lena, the Head Tracker, mused.

I had to admit that I was very proud of this meeting. Everything went smooth and we will be out of this pack's hair in a day or two.

"So, it's settled then. Atlas and I will be going to the Inn to talk to the owners now and will book all the rooms available." I dismissed the meeting and headed to my car with Atlas following me.

It only took a week before we were able to secure every room available for rent for our pack. We paid weekly to keep all payments up-to-date and in good standing. We knew there was a human employee who lived in the one suite connected to their front desk area, but that was okay. I mean, it's been six weeks and we had yet to see the person. I guess he was on a small leave of absence, but he would be back soon, at the least that's what the manager told me. She was excited for him to take back his overnight shifts she's been doing. Whatever; as long as he doesn't cause any trouble when he does resurface, I won't bother him any and neither will my pack.

Construction of our new house has started and though it's a slow process, it'll be worth it all in the end.

Chapter 3

We weren't allowed to move into the employee suite until I started working nights again, so today was moving day. I had been staying at the shelter with my son for five weeks as we were in the hospital Kenji's first full week of life. I was beyond ready to get him into a cleaner and safer environment. I woke up at 8 AM, but had only gotten a few hours of sleep the most. Kenji woke up a few times during the night for a bottle.

I was thankful it was a nice day out because I'd be walking two miles to get to the Inn from our shelter. No way in hell was I going to waste money on a taxi with this weather. Thank God the hospital gave me that stroller and car seat set. I woke up Kenji, fed him a bottle, changed his diaper, and then I changed him out of his pajamas. Since he was still a newborn, I put him in a long sleeve onesie and pants that had a dinosaur on the butt. Tiny socks for his feet came next. He looked so adorable. I was the luckiest dad in the world to have such a special boy.

I changed myself into one of my only pairs of jeans. They had so many holes, but not because of today's fashion. I've had them for years and tried my best to keep them in working condition. Now that I had Kenji, I had to make sure his needs and wants were met first. I threw on a plain black long sleeve shirt and slipped my only pair of shoes on, which were tennis shoes from the thrift store. I looked at myself in the shelter's bathroom and groaned at the dark mop I call my hair. It would forever stay messy.

I buckled Kenji into his car seat and then I connected it to the stroller. I laid the only baby blanket he has over him and pulled down the car seat's visor protecting him from the outside world and all its germs. When I was satisfied that he was secured, I started to gather up his wipes, diapers, formula, and bottles and threw them into my old backpack that officially became my new diaper bag. I slipped it onto my back and gathered all our clothes, which wasn't much. Kenji already had more than I did, but that's how it should be. We didn't even fill up a garbage bag's worth between us. Shame filled my body.

Kenji deserves so much better, I thought to myself. But I was too selfish. He was all I had and I was never going to give him up. I would die before that ever happened.

I shoved the bag of clothes into the basket connected to the stroller. In another bag, I shoved the few miscellaneous items we had that consisted of his baby monitor set, baby carrier, a few tattered paperback books, the tiny hat and swaddle blanket he first wore after his birth, a folder that holds important paperwork (his birth certificate, my birth certificate that Mom grabbed when we left our old life behind, Mom's death certificate, Kenji's bassinet card from his stay in the hospital nursery, and lastly, an award-like certificate that announces Kenji's birth with his weight, height, and has his handprints and footprints stamped on it), a folded picture of my parents and I together before Dad passed away, a picture of just Mom that I plan to give to Kenji when he's old enough to know the truth about his life, and lastly, Mom's urn with her ashes in it.

I didn't have keys or a phone, so I made sure that I had my wallet that simply consisted of my old driver's license, my son and I's Social Security Cards, and the last $30 to my name until I get my first paycheck after my leave. With the stroller loaded with my entire world in it, I grabbed Kenji's playpen that I had taken out of the box and was so relieved to find that it had a handle to carry when folded up. It was going to be a long walk with all this stuff in one trip, but I knew once I left this shelter in a few minutes, I'd never step foot in it again. With my head held high and my right hand firmly gripped to the stroller, I started walking Kenji and I towards our new life at the Arrowhead Inn.

Chapter 4

Here's our wolfie, River. Picture found on Google like always!

RAFFERTY MONTGOMERY

Yesterday was a shitty day and I'm still left in a bad mood from it. Nothing went right at the construction site and the Trackers hadn't gotten any new information in a few days. Not to mention, my wolf had been antsy the last few days. He was sure something was about to happen, but he wasn't sure what or if it was even good or bad. I was frustrated and pissed off; not a good combination for an Alpha who hasn't found his mate yet.

I knew I had to stay away from my members today. If I didn't, I was liable to snap and I didn't want that. So, I mind-linked Atlas and told him he was in charge today. He wanted to ask what was wrong, but decided against it, which was wise on his behalf. I love my best friend, but he didn't have a clue as to how I was feeling. I was alone when all I wanted was my mate. I wanted my mate more than anything. I went through my parents' deaths alone and now I'm going through this alone. I was so damn tired of being alone!

"Please, Moon Goddess, let me meet my mate soon!" River and I pray and beg. I wasn't ashamed to beg and plead for my mate. I would do absolutely anything to meet her or him. But then a thought hit me and I was left gobsmacked.

I was going to wage a war against whomever attacked my pack first. Now wasn't the time to meet my mate. My mate was safe and blissfully unaware of what's to come. As badly as I wanted my mate by my side, I forced myself to shove all thoughts pertaining to my mate to the very back of my mind. River was pissed at me for it, but even he understood where I was coming from. I was already one of the best Alphas in the United States. Finding my mate would make me even greater, but would also give my foes a vantage point, a weakness. Wolves are territorial, possessive, and protective creatures and that sometimes landed us in compromising situations.

I decided to outrun my thoughts by doing just that; going for a run. I was on our pack land already, so I pulled off my clothes and threw them down by a nearby tree. I rolled my shoulders back once before imagining myself as River. Almost instantly, I heard my bones breaking into bigger and stronger ones. I felt my wolf's fur spread all over my skin. Soon enough, I was on four legs instead of two.

Being an Alpha, my wolf was larger than most. River stood a little taller than a big grizzly bear. Our fur was a charcoal gray color with streaks and patches of white woven all throughout my body. My normally deep brown eyes have turned into my wolf's dark, icy blue color. My eyes so dark they almost looked black.

I must have ran at least ten laps around our borders. Seeing as we owned quite a bit land, I had been running for many hours. I was breathless, my muscles ached, and exhaustion was near, but I felt better. I felt recharged. So, yesterday was a bad day. We all had those. I wasn't going to give up on finding who burnt our house down. I made a vow I don't plan on ever breaking.

I shifted back to my human body once I was by the tree my clothes were thrown at. Quickly pulling them on, I made my way back to the Arrowhead Inn with plans to soak in their jacuzzi when I returned.

The combination of my long run and being relaxed and soothed by the spa would put me in a deep sleep, and that's exactly what I wanted tonight.

Chapter 5

The Arrowhead Inn is pictured above and found on Google. It's very nice, but not over the top. The color really matches its name and I love it.

KENZO CARSON

Our two mile destination had taken us over an hour to walk. When we got to the block the Inn was on, I nearly wept with joy. It took so long because I had pause and take some breaks. I was really out of shape and everything was heavy, but my determination was stronger. I was a daddy now and I wouldn't be weak anymore. I had someone worth fighting for with everything I had in me and I'll be damned if I ever stopped.

When we reached the hotel, I first noticed that the parking lot was extremely full, which normally wouldn't be weird, but it was 10:30 AM on a Monday. I haven't worked very many morning shifts, but even I knew this was strange. I was definitely going to ask Shelli about this. Shelli was my boss and co-owner of this fine establishment. She was great and I loved working for her and her husband. I was excited to see them again!

I took a deep breath and squared my shoulders. It was time to get settled in and talk to Shelli about taking over the maintenance man position. I had a lot to do and I still needed to make sure Kenji and I got a nap in later before my first overnight shift. I walked up to the automatic doors and through them once they opened.

I heard Shelli before I saw her. She squealed and came running out of the door that led to the workers' area. Knowing she'd want a hug, I sat Kenji's playpen down carefully and held open my arm for her. My reward was a hug and tight squeeze that nearly knocked me over, but I didn't care. It was the first affection I had been shown from someone other than Kenji since Mom died. I soaked it up because I never knew when I'd get another dote.

"Kenzo Carson, I am so happy to see that you're back! These night-shifts have been killer. Plus, I've just missed your cute little face around here!" Shelli enthusiastically greeted me. I furiously blushed when she called me cute. As if, I thought bitterly to myself.

"Thank you, Mrs. Conner. I am so glad to be back here. Thank you so much for letting Kenji and I live in the worker's suite. I swear you will never regret it." I promised her with a steely conviction.

"Kenzo, how many times do I have to tell you to call me Shelli? Mrs. Conner makes me sound so old! Anyways, it's our pleasure. You were a remarkable employee before everything happened, so it was a no brainer for us. Do you have time to chat after you get your things put away? There's a few things we need to talk about before your shift starts tonight."

I nodded eagerly and replied, "Yes, I was wanting to talk to you about something myself."

"Well, why don't you go to your room for a bit, settle in, and then check on Kenji? I will order us lunch and we can eat in the breakfast room in about an hour. I can't wait to meet Mr. Kenji later. I bet he's even cuter than his brot - I mean, his daddy." She said with a big smile.

My heart soared to the clouds and my chest puffed out in pride. She recognized me as Kenji's daddy. I glanced over to the car seat and looked at it fondly with a huge smile on my face. I heard Shelli clear her throat gently, so I looked back over to her and saw her hand outstretched with a silver key. She motioned for me to take it, so I did.

"Well, you know where your suite is and that's the key, so go along now. I will order us food and don't even think about trying to pay for yourself. This is partly a business lunch and will be paid for by me."

"Thank you, Shelli. Thank you for everything. We'll be back out here in an hour." I gave her one last hug that surprised her before I picked up the playpen and made my way towards Kenji and I's new home. Sure, it was just one suite in an inn, but it was ours, and that's all that mattered to me right now.

Chapter 6

D id someone just search for Beta Atlas? 'Cause his picture was just found on Google! Hahaha.

RAFFERTY MONTGOMERY

"Alpha Rafferty! We caught a rogue on the northeast borders!" My Head Warrior, Sam, mind-linked me. I was in the middle of digging the basement for our new pack house where the prison cells would be placed. However, the second I heard Sam in my head, I dropped what I was doing and shifted into River, my clothes be damned. Finally, FINALLY, we had caught our way to nailing a good lead onto whomever attacked us.

I sprinted as fast as my legs would go, but it still wasn't fast enough. Under normal circumstances, I didn't have an outright problem with rogues. Some were good, some were bad, I knew that. However, I wasn't in the mood to be so nonchalant right now. I was in the mood for answers and I was out for blood. Tonight, I'd be getting both. The thought filled me with a sadistic glee.

River was raging like a madman. He wanted to attack the rogue on site. It took a lot of persuading from me, but I managed to make him agree to letting me ask questions first. I promised him that he could have full control when the rogue was to be killed. I almost felt bad for the rogue. Almost.

A rancid odor filled my snout and it made River snarl. The scent of a rogue was a nasty stench that never failed to overwhelm my wolf's heightened sense of smell. I ran past the last of the trees and saw Sam, Atlas, and Lena surrounding the chained up feral wolf. The rogue had matted black fur covered in claw marks, which told me he had tried to attack and escape from my friends. Ha! One filthy rogue against three high ranking wolves from my pack? Not a chance in hell, but it'll make torturing him later even more fun. From the back of River's mind, I saw him making the creepiest and most vicious smirk ever.

I knew the rogue saw River's smirk because he started fighting against his restraints desperate to run away from the beast before him. His eyes were a dark red color laced with fear and anger at getting caught. River was satisfied for the time being, so I shifted back into my human body not giving a single fuck that I was nude. "Shift," I commanded in my angry and booming Alpha voice. My voice was so dominant that Sam, Atlas, and Lena dropped to their knees in submission after they had forced shift as well.

The rogue shifted into a man with tanned skin and a fairly fit body. He had short black hair that matched his wolf's matted fur. His eyes were a dull shade of green and he was glaring at me. I chuckled at his facial expression and watched him glare even harder.

"Should you be the one glaring here, mutt?" I asked, slightly amused, as a wave of dominance rolled off me. I saw the mutt trying to fight himself to not submit or answer me, but I knew he wouldn't win.

"Tell me, mutt. Why are you here and who sent you?" River spat out as I allowed him a little control. He was already mad, but the rogue's blatant disrespect edged him on even further.

The rogue just sneered and laughed at me. River snapped a bit causing me to slap the man across the face hard. The slap was so hard it turned his head to the side, left a handprint, and made an echo sound in the forest. I growled deeply and angrily enough to make everyone flinch.

"Tell me. Now." I demanded, allowing every ounce of power and dominance in my body into my words.

"Ashes to ashes, we all fall down." The man replied in a mocking tone. River pushed for control and I couldn't stop him. He drew the line at the disrespect towards what could have ended my pack's very existence. I grabbed the man's hands and crushed both of them with ease. His screams were music to River and I. If this man wanted to play games, games we would play.

I quickly stomped on his feet hard shattering the bones to pieces. The pain-filled screams encouraged River, but I pushed him back down. Answers were still needed before this rogue could be sent to hell.

"Do anymore bones need broken before we continue?"

The man, who was now on the ground writhing in pain, cried out, "n-no! I'll t-talk now."

"I thought maybe you'd change your mind eventually." I said with an evil grin. Time to get my answers, damnit.

Chapter 7

K enji's baby bellhop onesie! Isn't it so cute?! Special thanks to my special friend for giving me this idea by telling me it would be so cute to see Kenji in it. She's an amazing author, BTW, so go check her out. She's and you won't be sorry!

KENZO CARSON

With shaky hands, I managed to unlock the door to our suite. I walked inside to discover a king-sized bed, couch, and recliner. There was also a desk, dresser with TV on it, and a closet with a sliding door. Before entering farther, I opened up the bathroom door and peeked inside. There was a toilet and sink littered with travel-sized toiletries, a warm rack full of towels of different sizes, and a big bathtub that looked more like a spa with a movable shower head attached to the wall. I haven't had a good soak in the tub in years, so I nearly cried out in joy. Shutting the bathroom door, I pushed the stroller into the room further.

Once we get passed the short hallway to where all the furniture was, I looked to the left and was surprised to discover a mini kitchenette. There was a small oven, a sink, and a microwave. Glancing to the right, I saw a mini-fridge tucked into the corner. It truly wasn't much, but at least I would be able to save money by being able to cook for us.

I looked at the alarm clock that was perched on a nightstand next to the bed and saw that I had forty-five minutes before I needed to meet with Shelli. That was plenty of time to unpack everything, but first I wanted to check on Kenji, so I peeled the visor back and removed his baby blanket. Ocean blue eyes stared back at me. I smiled at him as I was unbuckling him. I scooped him into my arms and cradled him to my chest. Without even thinking about it, I kissed the top of his head and took a big sniff. Being six weeks old, his new baby smell was ever so present, and I loved it.

His diaper was feeling a little heavy, so I tugged his pants off and changed his diaper. I decided to feed him a bottle now with the hopes

I'd be able to eat my lunch warm later. After he was done suckling the bottle, I patted his back gently but firmly. A little burp made its way to my ears and I hummed in satisfaction. No tummy aches here, I cheered internally. I hadn't set up his playpen yet, so I carefully laid him swaddled up in his baby burrito position in the middle of the bed with pillows surrounding him, but they were a distance away because I was absolutely terrified of him smothering to death accidentally.

I quickly snatched up the playpen and set it up. Thank God it was an easy one where you just yanked up on all the sides and clicked them into place. Once I sat it up against the wall close to the bed, I gently grabbed Kenji and laid him down safely in it to nap while I quickly rushed around putting our belongings away. I glanced down at the clock and saw we only ten minutes before we needed to go back out, so I decided to disconnect the car seat from the stroller. I wasn't going to be leaving the Inn, so I settled on just carrying Kenji in his car seat. I sat the car seat on the bed and picked up Kenji and strapped him in. I made sure to grab the diaper bag and my new key before heading out front.

The mouthwatering smell of Thai takeout entered my nose and I inhaled a huge sniff. I loved Asian cuisine more so than any other type of food, but I very seldom got any. Walking faster, I made my way to Shelli and was ready to get down to business after I scarfed down my beloved Thai food. Without realizing it, I let a loud moan of pleasure. Shelli snickered at me as I felt my face flush with embarrassment.

"Thanks for lunch, Mrs- I mean, Shelli. It was scrumptious." I politely thanked my boss. She was my boss, that was a fact, but she was also my only friend.

"You're very welcome, Kenz. Now, I just wanted to inform you of the latest happening to our Inn. About a week after you went on your leave, I was approached by two men. Their large company mansion was burnt to the ground as a result of arson. They asked if they could book and rent out all our rooms for an indefinite amount of time. We agreed on a set rate. They get charged every Friday and all receipts need dropped under the boss's door." She told me all business-like.

Wow. This was something totally new. No wonder the parking lot was so damn full on a Monday morning. Well, maybe this wouldn't be so bad. I wouldn't have a lot of paperwork and computer work to do at nights, but that's fine. I would clean and organize things. And then my face paled when a thought hit me...

"Do they know Kenji and I live here now?" I nervously asked. What if they were mean or didn't like us? Even worse, what if they did like us and want to become friends?! What if they complained about Kenji and we got kicked out?! No, no. Stop it, Kenzo, and get a fucking grip, I scolded myself. Besides, no one ever wanted to be friends with me; not before Mom's ex-husband happened and definitely not now that he had scratched the surface unbeknownst to them, of course. Does Mom know what all he did to me now that she's gone? I frowned at that thought and hoped she didn't before shaking my head and forcing myself to focus on the matter at hand.

"They are aware and said they wouldn't bother you if you don't bother them." She smiled at me reassuringly.

"Okay then. This probably won't be so bad. Besides, I work nights, so I probably won't see many of them at all or very often." I tried to convince myself. It wasn't working, especially with the "who are you fooling?" face Shelli was giving me. Great. Fucking great.

"Kenzo, just relax. It's going to be fine and probably will only last a couple months while they rebuild a new company lodging. Oh! By the way, I have a present for Mr. Kenji, so why don't you get him out and I'll go grab it?" Shelli's entire demeanor changed instantly.

It's what I liked about her a lot. She went from boss mode to friend mode so easily.

I bent over in my seat and unbuckled Kenji from his car seat. The sudden movement must've scared him because he started crying even before he opened his little eyes. I cooed at him and rocked him gently. "Shh, my little love. It's just daddy. Just daddy. I got you, sweet boy. Daddy wants you to meet someone very special. Look, there she is!" Kenji calmed down with my soothing words and movements and that made me smile to myself.

Shelli came back just as Kenji calmed down and she was bouncing with excitement. When she saw Kenji, she held out her arms to hold him. Now, I knew it was just Shelli and she would never hurt my son, but I just felt this wave of over-protectiveness flood my body making me hesitate. No one else has ever held Kenji besides me other than the doctors and nurses at the hospital. At the shelter, we didn't have anyone bother us, so I never worried about this. Why was I feeling like this all of a sudden?

And then it occurred to me that it was going to be hard to let any woman hold him at all... because his own mother never got the chance. I swallowed a big lump in my throat and forced my unshed tears back into my eyes. Mom wouldn't want this, would she? No, she wouldn't. I don't think so, anyways. Why was this so fucking hard?

I heard Shelli saying my names prompting me out of my head. With shaky hands and an achy heart, I handed Kenji over to her. It wasn't fair to project my feelings onto Kenji and I most certainly didn't want him growing up afraid of women and not knowing how to treat them. She gently took him in his arms and immediately started gushing over him.

"He's a mini you already, Kenz. He's beautiful. Please, go ahead and open the gift."

I smiled and relaxed. This wasn't so bad after all. Besides, Shelli was the only person in my life other than her husband and my other boss, Scotty. Other women holding him would never be an issue because strangers would never get their dirty, grubby hands on him ever.

She slid the bag across the table and motioned for me to go ahead as she was lightly bouncing Kenji in her other arm. Excitement took over as I ripped open the bag and pulled out four identical baby onesies all in different sizes. When I unfolded them, I gasped and then starting giggling like crazy. Wait, when did I ever giggle? I'm a man!

A man who bottoms in his dreams and reads the same three erotic romance novels repeatedly, my conscious scoffed to me. I huffed to myself and went back to the moment.

"I thought since your little sidekick was going to be working with you that he needed a little uniform. I stumbled across these on accident, but I'm so glad I did. They're perfect! And I bought one in each size up to 12 months!" Shelli rambled on with a mixture of nervousness and excitement.

"I love them, Shell. Love them! Thank you so much! Kenji Michael Carson, get ready, son! You're going to be the cutest little bellhop to ever work in the hospitality business!" I raved and held the baby bellhop costume onesies to my chest. I loved them. She bought them, so he could wear them until he was too big for 12 month clothing. That meant Kenji and I would be here for the long-haul. We were safe and sheltered for a period of time I didn't have to worry about.

Chapter 8

Here's our fierce and beautiful Lena found on Google! She's a badass, just you wait and see!

RAFFERTY MONTGOMERY

"Tell me, now, who you're working for and what their plans are." My Alpha voice boldly demanded. I wasn't playing games anymore. I was a simple wolf; if I got my information quickly and without trouble, I killed quickly and painlessly. However, if trouble arose and a rogue refused, River got to appease his sadistic predatory side with a wicked delight. Of course, I wasn't a monster and neither was River, so we never harmed innocent rogues. We just captured and questioned them. Once we deemed them not a threat, we escorted them off our lands.

But right now, I just knew the piece of scum beneath my feet wasn't a lone wolf. No, he was up to something, and I intended to find out what using whatever means necessary. He didn't reply after five seconds, so I crouched down and held my face inches away from his. The stench made me want to go live in a Bath & Body Works store forever and that was really saying something because all the different scents gave me a headache. I felt my canines elongate and I slid my tongue across my teeth resulting in a murderous sneer. My silent demeanor was all it took for the thing to start talking out of sheer panic.

"It's the man who killed your parents. He wants to finish what he started!" The man nervously squeaked out. The mention of my late parents forced waves of anger to roll off of me in huge crashes. A vicious growl echoed all around us causing the leaves in the trees behind us to shake. I slapped the man across the face again and ordered him to continue.

"The man... h-he said that your brother ruined his l-life. That he was the rightful Alpha of the Burrow Hills Pack, b-but your grandfather gave it to your d-dad instead."

I took a minute to properly understand what I think the rogue was trying to say before spitting out through grit teeth, "Are you telling me what I think you're telling me? If you are, you better not be fucking lying or I will inflict so much pain on you that you will kill your pathetic self to escape from it."

I heard Atlas, Sam, and Lena gasp in shock. They had never seen this side of me before, but hell, neither had I. The rogue paled to a ghostly color and stammered out, "I-I'm not lying. H-he said your grandfather's name w-was J-Judas M-Montgomery-y and h-he was A-Alpha of the B-Burrow H-Hills P-Pack-k in K-Kansas City-y."

Clearing my throat so my voice wouldn't croak, I calmly asked, "What are you trying to say here, rogue? And choose your words very carefully. I want to hear the truth NOW!"

"Y-your father wasn't your grandfather's f-firstborn s-son. Your grandfather was having an a-affair and he got his mistress impregnated the same time h-he did your g-grandmother-r. The mistress gave birth the day before your f-father was born. J-Judas knew that his father would never let him take over as A-Alpha if he learned of his indiscretions, so he broke things off with his mistress and b-banished her from the pack. Y-your uncle grew up with feral wolves and watched his mother kill herself when he was 15... But h-he discovered a letter she wrote beforehand that held the t-truth and he vowed to avenge his m-mother's death and take back what was r-rightfully his."

"Give me his fucking name now, beast!"

The rogue smirked at me before saying, "Your u-uncle's name is go-fuck-yourself. You're as batshit crazy as he is. Guess it's a family thing."

All I saw was red. Red filled rage and red blood because I snapped the minute he said that and I ripped his ugly head off his grimy body like it was nothing. An angry, pain-filled howl rumbled out of my chest as I threw his head to the ground. Atlas, Sam, and Lena just stood there stunned from the revelation and from what they'd just witnessed. Not wanting to hear a damn thing from anyone, I closed off my mind-link from everyone and blocked my thoughts just to be safe.

The last thought I had before running off from my friends was, "Judas is a fitting name for a fucking traitor, isn't it?!"

Chapter 9

Here is Boss Lady, Shelli. So pretty! I love Jennifer Anniston, so I had to "cast" her somehow.

KENZO CARSON

"Oh, uh, Shelli? I have a question I'd like to ask if that's okay." I anxiously asked while my legs were bouncing up and down in a nervous twitch.

"Of course it is, Kenz. What's up?" She said with a curious smile gracing her face.

I took a deep breath before I blurted out, "I really want to save up money, but I can't with the one paycheck I'll be getting. I know Steve quit while I was on my leave and I thought I'd offer a solution. Since

I work as the night auditor, I have free time during the day. Could I take over the maintenance man position? Please?!"

Shelli cocked her head to the side and looked at me without saying anything for a couple minutes. I raised one eyebrow to encourage her to speak and she must have understood my cue because she straightened her posture and shifted to a more business-like position. "You know what? That's a great idea. But before I can promise you anything, I need to talk to Scotty. I'll let you know tomorrow morning when I relieve you from your shift. Does that sound good?"

"Yes! That will be fine! Thank you so much, Shell!" I exclaimed while jumping to hug her over the table. Kenji had fallen asleep as she was gushing over him, so I had put him back in his car seat about twenty minutes ago.

She chuckled and said, "It's no problem, Kenz. You're not just a valuable asset to our business; you're our friend, too. We want to help you all we can. Okay, I really need to go check how housekeeping has been doing, but I will see you at 9 for the start of your shift. Try to take a nap before then!"

She patted my shoulder after she had gotten up and started walking towards the Front Desk. Smiling to myself, I got up and threw all the takeout containers away before gathering up the diaper bag and Kenji. Not a bad day so far.

Once we got back to our room, I decided to take a bath while Kenji was still asleep. Relaxation was more important than a nap right now. I unbuckled Kenji from his car seat and quickly changed his diaper while he was still sleeping. After swaddling him up, I kissed his forehead softly and placed him in his playpen. I carefully took my shoes and socks off before heading towards the bathroom to start filling the tub with hot water. While it filled up with water, I emptied the mini bottle of bubble wash into the faucet stream. I made a mental note to go shopping for bubble bath soap for Kenji and for bath oils and bombs for me. I wasn't one to splurge normally, but we deserved a little something nice and this would be perfect for now.

I walked back out to the room and I pulled out a clean pair of boxer briefs that I tossed onto the bed for the time being. Mentally adding a laundry basket to my ever-growing list of items to buy, I just tossed my dirty clothes into the corner after stripping out of them. With one last glance at Kenji to make sure he was still out cold, I quickly walked to the bathroom. I decided to leave the door open a crack just to make sure I heard Kenji if he woke up and cried. Tears formed in my eyes at the beautiful sight in front of me; a big tub filled with jets, bubbles, and hot water just waiting for me to sit my naked ass down. I happily obliged as I stepped into the tub and sat down with a moan of pleasure and delight escaping my small mouth as the water welcomed my body. With my legs stretched out in front of me, I leaned my back against the tub and tilted my head backwards, so my face was looking at the ceiling with my eyes closed.

This was going to be the best hour of my life. I prayed to the Moon Goddess to let Kenji sleep through it - call me selfish, but I really needed a few minutes to collect myself. I knew it wasn't all about me anymore, but I was still only 22-years-old, going back to graveyard shifts after six weeks off of work, grieving my mother, and embracing life as the single, working parent of a newborn baby completely dependent on me for survival. It was a lot to cope with and handle, but my son was worth it all. I just wished I had more to give him right now. Someday, I'll give him the world; we just have to get there first, I promised myself determinedly. I would do whatever the fuck it takes to make sure that promise came true.

The Moon Goddess answered my prayer. After soaking in the hot water until it became cold and my body had turned into a raisin, I pulled the plug and got out. I dried myself off with a fluffy white towel and shook my hair causing water droplets to fly everywhere. Sliding on my clean underwear, I looked in the big mirror and sighed. I was so relaxed right now. I knew Kenji needed to wake up and eat because it was now almost three o'clock in the afternoon, so that is where I headed next.

Kenji cried when I woke him up, but he quickly calmed down when the bottle's nipple hit his little lips. He opened his mouth quickly and suckled away at his milk. I chuckled at how quickly he was able to be pleased. "Eat up, little man. You're gonna grow up to be strong. I'll make damn sure of it," I whispered to him as he ate away without a care in the world. I'm still astounded that the universe gave me the gift of him. Of course, I lost someone in the process, but that's life. It's always been unfair to me, but I refused to let anyone or anything take Kenji from me. He was my whole world and I knew I would never recover if anything ever happened to him.

Once he was finished with his bottle, I cradled him to my chest as I patted his back to get him to burp. "Come on, Kenj, burp for

Daddy," I cooed to my baby boy. "You don't want gas trapped in your tummy, son. You'll feel it later and you won't like it. Daddy really doesn't want to see you in any pain and discomfort," I added for good measure, even though I knew he didn't understand anything I said. A few more pats later caused a soft, long burp to escape his mouth. I grinned at him lazily and praised him with, "Good job, baby boy! I knew you could do it!" Kenji must have liked the pitch of my voice just then because he finally gave me his first little smile. And at that moment, nothing else in the world mattered more than making him smile again and again for the rest of our lives.

Chapter 10

As a sorry for taking so damn long to update, here's a picture of our sexy Alpha Rafferty thanks to good ole Google! Ugh, Nico Mirallegro is so easy on the eyes. Also, please, let me know what you think! Our two MCs are going to meet soon - eek!!!

RAFFERTY MONTGOMERY

Ignoring all the shouts and pleas from my friends, I shifted and ran away from them after blocking anything and everyone out. That rogue had to be lying... Right?! My grandfather was a great man of integrity. He was loyal. But maybe I just saw what he wanted me to see and I wanted to believe that it was true. I knew my father was a great man and Alpha; he loved my mother with everything in him and his pack was always on his mind. He did everything for us all. Wouldn't he have learned that from his father?

My grandparents and parents were all dead. I was all alone, except for my seemingly bloodthirsty uncle hellbent on revenge against his completely innocent nephew. I had my pack family, but I didn't actually belong to a family anymore because mine was all dead. Was this how my life was always going to be? Was I destined to be alone at the top? If so, I didn't want it. I didn't want it at all. I'd give it all up to find my mate because my mate was the last person I had and my last chance to belong to a family again. Unless he's dead already, I bitterly thought to myself.

River growled and snapped his jaw at me. Don't ever fucking think that again, Rafferty, or I won't be as nice next time, River snarled at me through our link. I winced at his threat, but he was right. That line of thinking wasn't going to help anything. Besides, now that I know about my "uncle," I really didn't want to find my mate until I killed that stupid son of a bitch. He killed my parents - truly innocent people - because of a grudge held against his father. He burnt down my home and caused my pack to panic. Uncle Dearest was going to fucking pay big time. For his sake, I hoped he was a masochist because

I was going to inflict so much pain on him repeatedly. I was going to torture him to the edge of death just to let him heal enough to do it all over again and again and again. I'd only stop when he begged for death; and then he'd have to kill himself because I sure as hell wouldn't end his suffering, and neither would my pack.

I ran for hours trying to escape my thoughts. I ran from Kansas City to St. Louis and back. Thank the Goddess I didn't accidentally stumble onto another pack's land. I was so caught up in escaping my troubles that I wasn't paying attention to borders like I should've been. I wasn't worried about humans seeing me because I was in my wolf form, so I just ran. It was a reckless run, especially for an Alpha, but I needed the adrenaline rush to take over my body and calm my thoughts for awhile. I needed a break.

It was 8:30 at night by the time I sauntered into the Arrowhead Inn's lobby. Pack members that were lingering in the lobby stopped and bowed their heads in greeting once they saw me. I shook my head. No matter how many times I've told my pack not to bow when we're alone, they never listened. I didn't want them to feel beneath me ever. Yes, there were rankings in our pack, but everyone was equal. My father made it that way because my grandfather was more old school and my dad didn't like it. I followed my dad's footsteps and kept everything the same way. Maybe that should have been an indication that my grandfather wasn't as great as I imagined him to be. Was I that stupid to not see it? Did my father know the truth? Did he keep me ignorant? Or would he have been just as surprised as I am now? I wish you were here, Momma and Daddy; I need you both so badly right now.

"Rafa! I'm so glad you made it back. We were worried about you, but we knew you needed time alone to process what that rogue said. Are you okay?" Atlas asked as he was flying down the stairs. He must've smelled me or felt my aura entering the hotel and rushed down like the great best friend he was. He was the closest person to me now and I don't know what I would do I ever lost him. He's more than just my Beta.

Atlas rushed towards me with open arms and I didn't hesitate in hugging him back. I was an Alpha, sure, but that didn't mean I was immune to human feelings of needing comfort and affection. I wasn't afraid to feel or show emotion and affection and I never would be. My parents raised me that way and I couldn't be more thankful for it.

"It was a lot to take in that's for sure. I really hope you, Sam, and Lena don't think I'm a crazed monster now. River took complete control and even though I couldn't stop him if I wanted to, I didn't want to stop him. What kind of Alpha loses control like that in front of his friends?!" I whispered horrified at what I had done earlier.

Loud laughter left my sensitive ears ringing, but I didn't care because it was Atlas. He eventually pulled himself together and pulled back from our embrace leaving his hands on my shoulders. "You know, Rafferty, for being one of the strongest Alphas in the world, you can be quite dense sometimes." River growled a bit at that remark, but I blocked him out relief flooded my system.

As long as my friends, because they were more than just my fellow high ranked wolves, thought I wasn't a monster, I would be okay. I wasn't my grandfather. I wasn't my uncle. I was my father's son and he was the man I aspired to be like.

We started walking towards the stairs when the faintest scent caught River's attention and he went crazy trying to force his way into control. Baby powder and cherry blossom flooded my nostrils and River's erratic behavior suddenly made sense... MATE!

MATE! MY MATE! FOLLOW THE SMELL AND GO TO MATE! River was screaming through our link.

But I couldn't. All I was focused on was...

Baby powder - no, just kidding! I wasn't one to make assumptions and jump to conclusions, so that didn't bother me at all. Besides, even if my mate had a baby with someone else, that wouldn't deter me at all, especially since I smelled that my mate was human.

What bothered me most of all was the impeccable timing the Moon Goddess had. I knew she had a plan for all of us, but couldn't she take our feelings into consideration at all sometimes? Now wasn't the time for my happily ever after. I had a pack house to rebuild and a murderous uncle to hunt down and kill before he attacked again.

Ignoring River's threats and Atlas's confused looks, I ascended the stairs and went to my room. I wasn't going to meet my mate yet for two reasons really. One: I needed a shower badly. I reeked, almost as bad as the rogue from earlier, and there was no way in hell I'd ever meet my mate like this willingly. Two: I was scared. Scared of rejection and scared of losing him or her. My mate was my last shot at belonging to a family again and I was completely and utterly terrified at the thought of losing that whether it was due to rejection or my

uncle.

Chapter 11

Greetings, my beautiful readers! I am so terribly sorry it took two months to update. I hit a really bad writer's block because I wanted Kenzo and Rafferty's meeting to be perfect and it took forever for me to find something I was okay with. Please, let me know what you think and I promise to update really soon as I know you're not gonna like where this chapter ends. As always, please enjoy our favorite daddy, Kenzo. Timothée Chalamet is so cute!

KENZO CARSON

Beep! Beep! Beep! I groaned as I lightly slammed my fist on the alarm clock. Kenji allowed us to get a good nap in before my graveyard shift. It was 8:00 now and I had one hour before my shift started. With one last groan, I forced myself to get up and ready. It was going to take longer than usual now that I had Kenji.

Before I woke up Kenji to feed him, I quickly dashed to the bathroom to relieve my bladder. I glanced at myself in the mirror as I washed my hands and sighed deeply. I was nervous about going back to work tonight not only of all the changes surrounding the Inn, but also because I'd have Kenji to take care of, too. What if I couldn't make this work? What if - don't go there, Kenzo. You have to make this work. You don't have a choice; Kenji is relying on you to make it. I shook my head to get my thoughts to clear as I grabbed my toothbrush and toothpaste that I would need to replace soon. I took one last glance in the mirror after I rinsed out my mouth and forced myself to smile and nod at my reflection. I was going to have to fake it till I make it for a bit.

After I fed and changed Kenji's diaper, I dressed him in his little bellhop onesie and socks. I strapped him into his car seat as I quickly threw on my uniform and packed the diaper bag. I was all set and it was time to head to work. I attached the car seat to the stroller and grabbed the carrier in case I needed it.

Shelli was anxiously awaiting our arrival as I made my way to the break room to clock in for my shift. She was standing up by the time I pushed Kenji to our spot behind the front desk. I situated his stroller to the side where it wouldn't be in my way if any guests needed help.

"Well, we weren't late for our first night back." I joked as I was trying to hide my nerves. Something felt different about tonight, but I could not decipher what it was and I was scared for when I finally did.

"You weren't late even when you lived two miles away and walked here," Shelli teased back. "So, since tonight is Thursday, you will have to charge out all the rooms via direct billing and then drop the receipts under room 201 as that is the boss's room. Mr. Montgomery pays in cash every Friday morning."

"Cash? For all of the rooms? Each week?" I questioned carefully.

"Yes, Kenzo, that's what I said."

My nose scrunched up at how unbothered she was. "You... You don't think that's kinda weird? Kinda sketchy? Like at all?"

Shelli sighed and looked at me, "Kenzo, it's been six weeks. We've had no issues with any of his crew and the FBI hasn't raided us yet. Mr. Montgomery is young and might just not be into credit cards. I don't know and I don't really care. He pays us and that's all that matters, okay? Don't go worrying about nothing now, hon." I nodded my head in response and bit my lip as I sunk into thinking.

Just how young is this Mr. Montgomery? I hated to admit it, but Shelli had me really curious about this man now, which was not good. I was known to crush easily and that's the last thing I needed, especially if he was a longterm guest at my place of work. Maybe she meant young as in her age and not mine! Yes, that is what I chose to believe.

"So, with that being the only thing different from your usual grave-yards, I'm gonna head home now. And yes, I'll talk to Scotty about the maintenance man position. Have a good night, Kenzo. I know you got this. And if you can't get everything done because of Kenji, don't worry. We know you two will have to find a system that works." Shelli said as she locked the door to their office and gathered her purse.

"Thank you. Thank you so much. I promise this will be worth it." I assured her and myself.

"I know that, Kenzo, but do you? Have some faith in yourself. You've always been a survivor, a fighter. Call us if you need anything, though, and I mean it. We'll come." She gave me a hug and kissed my cheek before gently tapping Kenji's car seat as a show of affection for him.

"You got it, boss. See you in the morning!" I was feeling better now. If my bosses had confidence in me, I needed to have confidence in me.

I peeked over at Kenji and noticed he had fallen asleep, so I took my chance to clean various places in the lobby without having to lug a baby around. Every time guests entered the sliding doors, I noticed they stopped and stared at me for a second before heading to their rooms. It made me feel awkward, but I just guessed they were accustomed to seeing Shelli or Scotty by now.

Eleven o'clock rolled around and Kenji had woken up crying. I quickly got him out of his car seat and started feeding him his bottle I had prepped a bit ago because I knew he was going to be hungry soon. As I was burping my son, I noticed a very handsome man heading outside, but he stopped in his tracks when he passed the front desk.

"Is it bring your kid to work day or something?" He smirked, but his eyes were sparkling, so I knew he meant no harm.

I chuckled and replied, "Every night will be that for me. My son and I are the ones living in the worker's suite and I'm allowed to bring him with me, so I don't have to worry about a babysitter."

The man's jaw dropped for a second as if he didn't believe what I had just said and I didn't blame him for it. It was kind of an absurd situation, but it was mine and I'd own it.

"Oh, shit. Man, now I kind of feel like an asshole for making a joke about it." He said with an embarrassed guilty look on his face.

"Guess it's a good thing I have an incredible sense of humor then, huh?" I teased back to show he was fine.

A deep laugh met my ears and it made me smile. "I'm Atlas, by the way. Second in charge of the company who's staying here. Guess I should've introduced myself first. Anyways, it's great to meet you, uh.."

"Kenzo. I'm Kenzo," I stated, "and this is my newborn son, Kenji." I proudly emphasized son for my own benefit. It still didn't feel real sometimes.

"Well, Kenzo and Kenji, it was a pleasure to meet you and I look forward to seeing you two more now. I better go now. My ma- wife is pregnant and she has a craving for some Kansas City barbecue."

"Pregnancy cravings are no joke, so you better go! We'll see you around, sir."

"Atlas! Just Atlas!" He hollered as he ran out of the doors into the night. I smiled and hugged Kenji. Maybe this wasn't going to be bad at all. If a man like Atlas was almost at the top of this company, Mr. Montgomery was bound to be even better. Right?

After changing Kenji's diaper, I strapped him into his baby carrier, so he could cuddle against my chest as I ran the night audit reports and could charge out the rooms for the week. I bounced my leg to rock him and he quickly went back to sleep. He was the best baby I ever could've asked for and I placed a kiss on his head before getting to work.

I had all the receipts ready to be dropped, so I stood up, transferred the phone to the walkie talkie, and headed to the stairs to slide them under Mr. Montgomery's door. I was worried the elevator would awake Kenji and I needed him to be asleep and quiet in the hallways.

With every step upward, my heart pounded harder in my chest and I couldn't figure out why. Eventually, I just summed it up to being nervous Kenji would cry or scream any second. I finally got to the top and opened the door that led into the second floor hallway.

I was right across from room 201. I walked over to the door and crouched down to slide the receipts underneath only I was stopped.

Stopped by the sound of locks unlocking and a door being opened...

Shit, maybe I wasn't as quiet on the steps as I thought. I gulped and slowly trailed my eyes up the body of the most gorgeous man I had ever seen...

And I promptly fell onto my butt in humiliation when I met his dark brown eyes and furrowed eyebrows cocked at a dangerous angle.

Chapter 12

The television was on, but I wasn't watching it. I was too far gone imagining the person behind the baby powder and cherry blossom smell. There was an easy solution to this, but I was being stubborn. Atlas had asked if I wanted to make a food run with him and while I was starving, I had no desire to entire that hotel lobby.

"For an Alpha, you sure are a coward," River pushed through our mind link. I scoffed and rolled my eyes. He was such an asshole sometimes.

"I just met the human who lives here." Atlas mind-linked me. My head snapped up and I didn't know what to say back. "He has a baby boy he brings to work with him." My intrigue in my mate skyrocketed. My mate is a man (thank the Moon Goddess for that part at least). A human man with a human baby. I was filled with endless questions and curiosities now.

"He's funny, too, Rafa. I think you'll like him. I know I already do!" Atlas mind-linked me again. A rush of pride filled me. My Beta was already feeling loyalty to his Luna and he didn't even know it yet.

"Thanks for the info, At. I'll probably meet him in the morning when I pay for the rooms. Get back safely." I finally said back and then blocked off my mind. I needed alone time to think.

Baby powder. Cherry blossoms. I was thinking about my mate so much I felt like his scent was getting stronger and closer each second. And then I heard footsteps so soft on the stairs and I knew. I knew that was him. My heart was pounding and my breathing was heavy because I wasn't sure what to do.

I heard him enter the hallway and close the door to the stairs as quietly as he could. I even heard him take a deep breath and that is when I just couldn't fight the mate pull anymore. I needed to see him.

Out of pure instinct, I quickly unlocked my door and opened it only to feel my breath leave my body entirely. My mate was more beautiful than I could have ever imagined. He was perfect, angelic, a masterpiece. The baby was too small for me to see in the carrier, but I somehow knew he was just as beautiful as his dad and the thought made my wolf puff out in pride at our future pup.

Just feeling his eyes trail up my body and hearing him gulp made my brown eyes darken and my eyebrows arch. Fuck. One second in and I was a goner and I didn't know how I'd ever fight it. We finally locked eyes at last and then he fell onto his butt in surprise at being caught.

We stared at each other for five minutes before a little cry broke us of our trance. My mate turned red and began to soothe his baby. I held out my hand to help him up and he slowly took it. Sparks flew up my arm in a sensation I've never felt before, but was already wanting to feel again. I knew my mate felt them also by the way he with gasped and withdrew his hand immediately.

"S-sorry, sir. I was just dropping your receipts off and thought I was being q-quiet. Here they are, but I need to go before Kenji bothers anyone." My shy mate said before thrusting the papers in his hands at me and hurrying down the stairs.

I was in shock for a minute and didn't know what to do. He was already so much more than I ever imagined, but the timing was horrible, especially since he had a baby. River, however, didn't care. He wanted to formally meet our mate, so he pushed for control and I was left running after the man with the baby.

When I pulled myself together enough to enter the lobby, my eyes darted to the front desk where I knew he'd be. Sure enough, I saw him making a bottle with shaking hands, which made me frown. Was he upset over what happened? Through the small start of our mate bond, I felt anxiety and nerves rolling off him in waves and my wolf yearned to help our mate, but he also knew we had to take things slow.

Not wanting to startle him any further, I cleared my throat and watched as his head snapped up in my direction. Once he saw me, he quickly diverted his attention back to the bottle. The baby was fussing around still, but he wasn't crying like he was upstairs. I waited and watched him as he cradled his baby in his harms and began to feed him. After watching a few suckles, I decided it was time to formally meet my mate - the man I've been waiting for four years.

"Hi, I'm Rafferty Montgomery. I just wanted to make sure you two were okay," I said. At the mention of my name, I saw my mate's eyes widen and his jaw drop. Had he heard of me before?

"Shelli wasn't kidding when she said Mr. Montgomery was young," he mumbled to himself, but he didn't know of my heightened werewolf senses.

"That she was not," I mused back with a grin and he sheepishly smiled back.

"I'm Kenzo Carson and this is my baby boy, Kenji. Thanks for checking on us, sir, but we're fine, I promise," he croaked out nervously. "I'm also sorry if we bothered you. I tried so hard to be quiet and I'm sorry you had to get up."

"Don't apologize, Kenzo. You didn't do anything wrong at all. It was just a coincidence of sorts that will make sense later, I reckon." I responded with a small smile for extra reassurance.

Kenzo looked down at Kenji and was quiet for a few minutes before speaking up. "Uh, sir? Is there anything I can help you with? I'm almost done feeding him if you don't mind waiting. I can give you a couple coupons for free drinks during our happy hour tomorrow for your time."

It was easy to tell that my mate was very overwhelmed and I hated that. He was supposed to be calm around me, his mate, but that would come later after we complete the mating bo- no, no, no. Don't fucking go there, Rafferty, or else you'll pop a boner in no time.

"I really don't mind waiting. Take your time. So, did you enjoy your time off work?" I asked wanting to know more about my mate. His face dropped after he heard my question and I immediately felt bad. "Never mind, Kenzo. That's none of my business." Yet, I thought to myself.

He relaxed a bit, but didn't look back up at me and it actually made me kind of sad. I wanted to look at his face and memorize the beauty of it. He was stunning and I just knew he didn't think so. I'd have to change that and I would. Eventually. After I captured my crazy uncle and took his life.

Kenzo burped Kenji and had rocked him to sleep, so I watched as he put him back into the carrier strapped to his chest.

"Okay, Mr. Montgomery, what can I do for you now?" He asked while reaching for those happy hour coupons he promised me earlier.

"Mr. Montgomery is my dad. Please, call me Rafferty. I'm not old yet!"

Kenzo laughed and nodded his head in agreement.

"I actually didn't need anything. I just wanted to introduce myself since we'll be seeing a lot of each other for awhile," I finally admitted.

"Oh, okay. Well, thank you for that." Kenzo said back dismissively. River growled internally at that, but I shoved him down and told him to behave.

"You're welcome. I'm gonna head back to my room now and get some sleep, but I'll be down in the morning to pay for the rooms. Nice meeting you, Kenzo. Oh, and you, too, Kenji!" A smile etched its way onto my face as I waved goodnight to my mate and pup.

"You know where to find me in the morning," Kenzo retorted. I was starting to think this man was a bit of a brat, but time would tell. I'd just have to wait and see.

Chapter 13

KENZO CARSON

"You know where to find me in the morning."

The second Rafferty turned his back, I scrunched my nose and dropped my head. What the hell was that, Kenzo? You know where to find me? I was so mad at myself. This gorgeous and nice man probably just thought I was rude now. But it didn't matter if he did because I was not here to make friends. Although, the thought of never getting to know him more made my heart drop a bit. He's too handsome to ever want someone like me in his life and it wasn't very likely he was even gay, not that it mattered to me any.

I shook my head and forced myself to push all thoughts of Rafferty to the back. There was still over half my shift left and I had things to do before morning arrived. Since Kenji was back to sleep, I decided to fold the last two loads of freshly cleaned towels. Call me crazy, but I actually really liked folding towels. The repetitive motion was soothing to me.

The rest of the night passed by rather quickly between taking care of Kenji and finishing my duties. It was almost seven in the morning and I was starting to get antsy because I didn't know when Rafferty would be down to pay his bills. I knew it was stupid, but I really wanted to see his beautiful face again. I was going to allow myself the privilege of looking and admiring him from afar, but I wouldn't befriend him or anything.

"WHAT DO YOU MEAN THERE ARE NO ROOMS AVAILABLE FOR THE FORESEEABLE FUTURE?!" An angry guest on the phone yelled at me. Rude people were something I didn't miss at all in my absence.

"Ma'am, I'm sorry, but we don-" CLICK. The caller hung up on me and I sighed as I put the phone down.

"Rough morning?" A smooth voice asked. I looked up and saw Rafferty staring at me with a small smile.

"Just getting yelled at for having no rooms available." I admitted with an involuntary eye roll. "Are you ready to pay your bill, sir?"

"Kenzo, we look to be the same age. Sir is not necessary. Rafferty is my name - please, use it."

I didn't know why, but I felt relieved that he wasn't so high strung for a man our age in a position like his. He seemed really grounded and down to earth, which I liked a lot to my dismay.

"It looks like it'll be $21,000 for the week." I said as my eyes grew large. He's been paying this every week? Wow. Yeah, he's way, way out of my league for sure.

Rafferty pulled his wallet from his back jeans pocket and opened it up. He pulled out a wad of cash and held it out to me. I tried to slyly bite my lip to calm my nervousness as I reached out to the money. Of course, I fumbled a bit and my fingers brushed against his hand as I grabbed the bills. Sparks overwhelmed me like they did last night and I pulled my hand back in shock causing the bills to fly everywhere.

With a red face, I quickly blurted out, "oh, my God. I am so sorry, Rafferty. So sorry. Just let me gather it up and I'll count it, so, you can get on with your day. I'm sorry to stall you like this." And just as

I began to shakily pick up the money, Kenji started to cry at the top of his lungs. I was mortified.

My head dropped in shame as I began to realize that I was failing. I couldn't work and take care of Kenji at the same time. Tears welled up in my eyes and I furiously blinked them away as now was not the time to show more weakness.

"Kenzo, please, stop apologizing. It was an accident. Here, I'll pick up the money, you check on your baby, and then maybe we can switch while you count if you feel comfortable with that?" Rafferty calmly asked and took control of the situation. It was oddly reassuring and relief flooded my body, which scared the crap out of me. This man, although very sexy and kind, was a stranger! Where did these weird feelings come from?

To save myself from further embarrassment, i meekly nodded my head and turned to get my son. I had just changed and fed him right before I got that rude caller, so, I wasn't sure why he was crying. But it quickly became apparent that he just wanted held because as soon as he was snuggled into my arms and cradled to my chest, my baby boy settled down and stopped crying. He did, however, give himself the hiccups.

"Shh, Kenji, it's okay, baby. Daddy's here." I murmured to him as I rocked him. I zeroed in on Kenji as I heard Rafferty collecting the hundred dollar bills, but I was too humiliated to look at him right now. My face was bright red and hot and I really didn't want him to see me like this.

I heard Rafferty say my name to get my attention. As much as I wanted to stay looking at Kenji, I knew I had to be professional and do my job. So, I took a deep breath of dread and looked back up to the man across from me. There was no malice in his eyes, no annoyance or frustration. He just looked at me with compassion and understanding. To say I was surprised was an understatement and I felt really guilty about that.

"Thank you, Rafferty, for being so kind and accommodating right now. It won't always be like this, I promise." I said in a composed and polite manner. He was be so gracious and I needed him to know I appreciated it and that I would be better next time. For some reason, I just really didn't want him to think I was inept or incompetent.

"It's no big deal, Kenzo. You can relax. I'm not a Karen," he joked with me. And I laughed at that pretty hard. I didn't have a phone, but that didn't mean I never used the computers at work during my downtime.

"Right you are. Wanna switch? I've got Kenji relaxed now." I was nervous about letting a stranger hold Kenji, but Rafferty has proven he's a good guy and we'd be seeing him a lot as it inevitable not to. Maybe we'd be friends. Just friends. Nothing more.

Kenji poked his little eyes open as I handed him off to Rafferty whom appeared to be nervous that he'd cry again. Rafferty looked a bit stiff trying to find the right way to hold little Kenji in his muscular arms, but he was also gentle. It was kind of amusing to watch. Kenji cuddled into Rafferty's chest finally and closed his eyes. A smile full of relief graced Rafferty's face and I almost forgot that I had a job to do that involved counting out $21,000 in cash.

Wow. I wondered what his company was that made him able to afford this while also rebuilding a new lodging place all at once. I quickly counted out the exact amount and was able to complete the transaction.

"Okay, Rafferty sir, you are good to go. Thank you for holding Kenji while I counted the money and for your patience. I'm sure Shelli was much quicker at this than I am." I held my arms out to get my son

back. Rafferty placed him carefully in my arms and was very cautious

of not touching me at all. Did he feel the sparks, too? Or was it my

imagination running wild?

"Kenzo, if I may, you need to give yourself more credit and more time

to adjust before you admonish yourself so much. You're doing so

much more than anyone else our age and it can't be easy. I do need

to get running now, though. I need to check on the construction

site." He said in a business manner. I was a little taken aback how

quickly he could switch modes just like Shelli. Was that a business

owner trait?

"Of course. Have a good day and thank you for choosing the Ar-

rowhead Inn!" That made Rafferty release a deep chuckle as he left

through the sliding doors and I knew then that I was in trouble. Big

trouble. Two interactions with this man and I was already starting

to feel a way I never had before.

www.ingramcontent.com/pod-product-compliance
Lightning Source LLC
Chambersburg PA
CBHW071356200726
48294CB00004B/1185